Feathers

Contents

Chapter One
The Birthday Mystery   2

Chapter Two
The Mix Up   10

Chapter Three
Too Many Birds!   17

Chapter Four
Feathers Are Fine   24

Chapter One
The Birthday Mystery

Mario knew he shouldn't have been listening at the kitchen door, but Mum and Dad were whispering. It made him curious.

"No dogs or cats," he heard his mother say. "You know I'm allergic to them."

His parents had forgotten about whispering, so Mario could hear every word they said. What could they be talking about?

Then Dad said, "Does it have
to be a pet? Can't we get him
a computer game or something?"

"That's what we got him for his
seventh birthday," replied Mum.

So that was it. His present. Mario quickly tiptoed away down the hall and ran outside.

Avis, his sister, was peering under the garden bushes.

"Now look what you've done," she grumbled. "You've scared that baby blackbird into the neighbours' garden, and their cat might get it."

"So what?" Mario muttered. He didn't like birds. They were creepy.

He changed the subject.

"Mum and Dad are talking about what to get me for my birthday. I think it's a pet."

"What kind of pet?" asked Avis.

Mario shrugged.

"You know what Mum and Dad are like. It has to be a surprise. Maybe *you* can find out what my present's going to be."

"A small animal," Avis told Mario the next morning.

"A guinea pig? A mouse?" asked Mario.

"I'm not sure," Avis replied, "but I think it's a rabbit. I saw Mum looking at a plan for some kind of hutch."

"Are you sure it was a rabbit hutch?" Mario asked eagerly.

"I'm pretty sure," she replied.

Mario felt good about getting
a rabbit. He spent lots of time
playing with the one at school.
It was cuddly, and he loved
to hold it.

The trouble was if you wanted to
take care of the rabbit, you also
had to take care of the canary.
And he hated the canary.

That night, Mario lay awake
wondering what colour his rabbit
would be and what he would
name it.

Chapter Two
The Mix Up

Each year, Avis and Mario took turns having either a big birthday party with lots of kids, or a family party.

This year, it was Mario's turn for a family party, and it was just as well no one else came!

They'd finished hamburgers, then cake and ice cream, and it was present time. Everyone gathered, and Mario opened his gifts.

"I'll get our present now,"
Dad said. "It's still at the shop.
We couldn't bring it home any
sooner – that would have spoiled
the surprise."

Mum walked into the kitchen,
and Avis nudged Mario, grinning.

At last, Dad's car pulled
back into the driveway. As Dad
came in with the box, Mario saw
him give Mum a strange look.
Mario was a little bit puzzled,
but he didn't have time
to worry about it.

"Thanks, Dad!" Mario said.
He quickly lifted the lid of
the box and looked in.

But there was no rabbit. Instead,
something fluttered up into Mario's
face. It flapped madly around
the room and finally came to rest
on the window sill.

Mario backed into the corner, covering his face with his hands.

"It's OK, Mario," Dad said. "It's only a little rooster. It's called a bantam, and he's more frightened than you are. There's a hen in the box, too."

He picked up the rooster from the window sill. Its eyes were like glass and a red comb flopped around on top of its head.

"Where's... the rabbit?" Mum said. She looked surprised.

"There was a mix up at the pet shop," Dad said, still holding the rooster. "They'd sold it."

Mario couldn't stay in the living room with those birds. He ran to the door and stumbled into his bedroom. He didn't want anyone to see the tears streaming down his cheeks.

Chapter Three
Too Many Birds!

The next morning, Mario looked out his bedroom window at the rabbit hutch in the backyard. Avis was slipping chicken feed through the wire netting.

The rooster made excited noises, then it stood back while the hen ate. The neighbours' big cat watched from up on the fence.

"Come and see them, Mario," Avis called. "They won't hurt you!"

Mario walked away from the window. He'd never told anyone how he felt about birds, but Avis had seen him with the school bird.

"Well," Dad said at breakfast, "if you don't want the bantams, Avis can have them."

For the next week, Avis spent all her spare time fussing over the bantams. She named them Ginger and Rocky. Mario stayed as far away as he could. The birds would take over. He just knew they would.

The birds took over even sooner than Mario expected. Avis made a fuss about Ginger and Rocky needing more room, so they were allowed out in the garden for a while each day.

"Ginger's laid another egg," Avis reported almost every day.

At the end of a week, she announced, "Ginger didn't come out with Rocky this morning. She must be sitting."

Now Mario was sure that in a few weeks there would be even more birds running around in the backyard.

In three weeks, five eggs hatched.
The chicks were yellow like fuzzy
little bumblebees on toothpick legs.

After school one day, all of Avis' friends came to see the chicks. Mario watched them from his bedroom window as they crowded around the cage full of bantams and bantam babies.

Mario lay on his bed to read, then he heard Ginger clucking. The clucking got louder and louder. He looked out the window. Ginger and Rocky were just below him, scratching around in the bushes.

"Someone must have left the cage door open," Mario said softly. "Well, it's not my problem."

Then something made him look
towards the fence. Crouched on
the top was the big cat from next
door. It was staring down at the
bantams and the five chicks!

Chapter Four
Feathers Are Fine

With a sudden spring, the cat landed very close to Ginger.

Spreading her wings, Ginger turned to face the cat. Then, with her neck stretched out and beak open, she ran at the cat! The cat backed off towards the fence and crouched, tail twitching.

Mario was surprised to find himself banging on the window and shouting, "Watch out, chickens!"

Mario raced outside. Rocky had run back into the cage, but Ginger was still herding her chicks towards the open door – and the cat was right behind her.

"Now what do I do?" Mario wondered. "I'll have to grab the cat, but that might scare the chicks, and they'll scatter. But if I don't do something, it'll be too late."

Mario didn't have time to think. At that moment, the cat sprang, missing Ginger only by a feather. By the time the cat landed, Ginger and the chicks had reached the safety of the cage.

For the first time, Mario went up to the cage and peered in at the chicks. None of them looked hurt. Their mother had saved them just in time.

"You're a smart bird, Ginger,"
he said as he shut the door. Wait
a minute! There were only four
chicks in the cage. One was still
out there — somewhere!

The cat was crouching, dead still,
staring into the bushes. The tip of
its tail twitched.

Mario stared into the bushes, too.
Leaves quivered, and the missing
chick scuttled across the garden.
At first, it seemed that the tiny
bird was heading straight for the
cat, but as the claws lashed out to
gather it in, the chick swerved,
and not a moment too soon!

In a second, Mario had it in his hands. Under the fluffy down, he felt its heart beating.

"Poor little thing," he said.

Holding it against his chest, he stroked its head with one finger.

He was surprised. The chick didn't feel one bit like feathers! Then he put it in the cage.

"You're a clever little chick," Mario told it, "and brave."

He almost reached in to pat it – but not quite.

He was still crouching quietly by the cage when Avis came back.

"What are you doing?" she asked, looking surprised.

"Just rescuing one of our chicks from the neighbours' cat!" Mario said happily.

From the Author

Some children are scared of spiders, some of the dark. When our granddaughter received a bantam hen as a present, we discovered she was scared of birds!

Marie Gibson

From the Illustrator

I used to draw comic strips and illustrate T-shirts and blankets. This led me to illustrating children's books, which I have been enjoying for the past eight years.

Richard Hoit